I0523824

A Dragon Hatched!

JENNI WARD

First published in 2025
by Miraworth Books
ABN 44 964 848 123

Copyright © Jenni Ward 2025

The right of Jenni Ward to be identified as the author of this work has been asserted by her in accordance with the Copyright Amendment (Moral Rights) Act 2000.

This work is copyright. Apart from any use as permitted under the Copyright Act 1968, no part may be reproduced, copied, scanned, stored in a retrieval system, recorded, or transmitted, in any form or by any means, without the prior written permission of the publisher.

MIRAWORTH BOOKS
PO Box 3523, Mount Gambier, SA 5290, Australia

ISBN (e-book): 978-0-6458856-9-9
ISBN (paperback): 978-0-6458856-8-2

Cover Design by Miraworth Designs

Contents

Chapter 1

The Glowing Egg

The Easter eggs were everywhere. Purple ones peeked from behind rose bushes. Yellow ones sparkled in the morning sun near the old oak tree. Pink ones had rolled under the park bench where Mrs Carson was reading her newspaper.

Naomi crouched beside a patch of daffodils. She pushed her curls away to see better. There it was! A spotted egg. "Found one!" She picked up the blue egg and dropped it into the wicker basket she shared with her best friend.

"I see three more by the fountain!" Kellie called out, her red ponytail swishing as she raced across the grass. She was always the faster runner, but Naomi was better at spotting the tricky hiding places.

The girls had been hunting Easter eggs in Burton Park since sunrise. Their basket was heavy with chocolate eggs wrapped in shiny foil. Naomi counted fifteen. Kellie said there were sixteen, but she might have counted the plastic one twice.

"Wait." Naomi stopped walking. She tilted her head, her gaze studying the fountain. "Do you see that, Kellie?"

"See what?" Kellie bounced on her toes, looking around.

"Over there." Naomi pointed carefully. "Between those two pink eggs."

Behind the fountain, next to two ordinary pink eggs, sat something different. This egg was bigger than the others and seemed to glow with a soft green-blue light. The shell looked smooth as river stones, and tiny sparkles danced across it.

The girls walked over to have a better look.

"It's not like the others." Naomi put the basket on the grass.

Kellie dropped to her knees between the basket and the eggs. Reaching out, she touched the biggest egg.

"Whoa! It's warm!" She looked up at Naomi. "Easter eggs aren't supposed to be warm, are they?"

"Not unless they've melted!"

Kellie touched it again. She shook her head. "Not a gooey egg."

"Hmm, strange. It looks like it's glowing," Naomi said. She knelt down too. Naomi wanted to touch the egg but didn't. "Maybe we should tell someone about this."

Before they had a chance to move, the egg began to wobble. A small crack appeared near the top, then another. The glow grew brighter.

"It's hatching!" Kellie shouted.

"But that's impossible," Naomi whispered. "Easter eggs don't—"

A tiny green-blue snout poked through the shell. Then came two big golden eyes, blinking in the sunlight. The creature inside wiggled. Then it pushed against the egg with its tiny hands. Once. Twice. On the third push, the rest of the shell fell away.

Both girls sat up straight. It was definitely not a chocolate bunny.

The baby dragon was no bigger than Naomi's hand. His scales shimmered like ocean waves, changing from deep green to bright blue as he moved. Two tiny wings fluttered on his back, and his tail had a small

fin at the end like a fish.

"Oh my," Naomi

breathed.

"Oh WOW!" Kellie

practically yelled. "It's

a real dragon! A tiny,

perfect dragon!"

The dragon looked up at them and opened his

mouth. Instead of fire, he let out the tiniest sneeze.

Glittery mist puffed from his nose and swirled around

the girls' feet.

Then the world began to spin.

The park, the fountain, even Mrs Carson with her newspaper, all started whirling faster and faster. The glittery mist grew thicker, lifting Naomi and Kellie off their feet. Their basket of Easter eggs spun with them, chocolate eggs flying everywhere.

"What's happening?" Naomi asked.

"Hold on!" Kellie grabbed Naomi's hand.

The baby dragon gave another small sneeze, and the spinning became a wild, rushing wind. Up, up, up they went and were carried away from everything they knew.

Chapter 2

Welcome to Dreyana

The whirlwind stopped as suddenly as it had started.

Naomi's feet finally touched solid ground. Her stomach

still felt like it was spinning, but the world had stopped

moving.

She blinked. Then blinked again.

They weren't in Burton Park anymore.

Floating islands drifted through the sky above them,

each one trailing ribbons of water that fell like upside-down rain. Purple and silver flowers, as tall as Naomi, glowed softly in the grass around her feet. In the distance, mountains made of what looked like crystal caught the light and threw rainbows everywhere.

"Kellie," Naomi whispered. "Are you seeing this?"

Kellie sat up slowly, brushing sparkly grass from her jacket. Her mouth hung open. A butterfly the size of a dinner plate fluttered past her nose. Its wings looked like stained glass windows.

"This is AMAZING!" she finally said.

The baby dragon rolled out of their basket and shook himself like a tiny dog. Their chocolate eggs lay scattered everywhere, but he barely looked at them. Instead, he spread his tiny wings and took a wobbly hop towards some singing flowers.

"Welcome to Dreyana, little ones."

The voice came from above. A big d r a g o n landed softly in front of them, her  golden scales gleaming like warm honey. She was huge compared to their tiny friend, but her golden eyes looked kind.

"I am Embera," she said gently. "And you have brought home someone very special."

Naomi found her voice first. "We're not dreaming, are we?"

"Dreams rarely have chocolate eggs scattered across magic meadows," Embera chuckled. She looked down at the baby dragon, who had stopped chasing flowers and was now studying her. "Though this little fellow might disagree."

The baby dragon sneezed, and tiny bubbles floated from his nose instead of glitter. He seemed surprised by this, tilting his head to watch the bubbles drift away.

"He keeps doing that," Kellie announced, jumping to her feet. "Is he sick or something?"

"Quite the opposite." Embera smiled. "He's a Tide Dragon. The sneezes mean his powers are waking up. Though they usually wait until a dragon is at least a week old."

"A Tide Dragon?" Naomi repeated carefully.

"Born only once every hundred years," Embera explained, settling onto the grass like a cat. "Their job is to keep our magic oceans calm and flowing right."

The baby dragon waddled over and tried to climb onto Embera's back, chirping happily. But when she mentioned oceans, he paused, his tiny head turning towards the distant sound of water.

"Have you blessed him with a name yet?" Embera asked.

The two girls looked at each other. Both thought hard about what name suited the little dragon best.

"His name is Bluey!" Kellie declared. "Don't you think that suits him, Naomi?"

"Bluest of all blues. Perfect name." Naomi looked over at Bluey as he looked closely at Embera's scales.

"Bluey," Embera repeated. "A very fitting name."

"Why was Bluey in our world?" Bluey glanced towards Kellie as she spoke.

She lowered her great head closer to the girls. "A terrible mix-up. This little one was never meant to end up in your world at all."

"OH NO!" A shimmering bird crash-landed right in the

middle of their circle, feathers flying everywhere. "I found you! I've been looking everywhere! This is TERRIBLE!"

Chapter 3

The Starling of Tides

The bird's feathers shifted between deep blue and sea foam green, like waves rolling onto shore. He hopped around frantically, bumping into Embera's tail and nearly stepping on Bluey.

"Calm down," Embera said gently. "This is the Starling of Tides, girls."

"I dropped it!" the Starling wailed. "I was supposed to carry the egg to the Sacred Pools, but I saw some really pretty clouds and—SPLASH—right through a portal to the human world! Then I got distracted by flying fish and forgot until this morning!"

Bluey tilted his head and let out a tiny roar. He blew a stream of bubbles at the flustered bird, who tried to pop them with his beak.

"The egg wasn't the only thing you dropped, was it?" Embera asked.

The Starling's feathers drooped. "The Tide Crystal too. It was supposed to be placed in the shrine when the little one hatched."

"Let me explain this to our guests and the missing egg," Embera said.

The Starling tilted his head. "Egg? Where?"

"Oh, he's silly. Bluey was in the egg," Kellie said.

"That is good news. That one is found." The Starling settled down next to Embera.

"Let me begin," Embera said.

As Embera explained what had happened, Bluey's behaviour changed. The playful look faded from his face. For a moment, he sat on Embera's scales, near her wings. Then he climbed down from her back and sat very still, his golden eyes fixed on her as he listened.

When she pointed towards the distant mountain that sparkled like diamonds, Bluey turned to look. His gaze wasn't just curious now—it was focused. Something about that faraway peak called to him.

"The Tide Crystal was supposed to be placed in the shrine when Bluey hatched," Embera continued. "The crystal helps focus his powers so they don't get out of control."

Naomi frowned. "What happens if his powers get

out of control?"

"Floods," Embera said seriously. "Terrible floods that could wash away entire islands."

At the word 'floods,' Bluey's whole body went stiff. His scales, which had been a gentle blue-green, suddenly flashed brighter. He looked around at the beautiful floating islands, the singing flowers, the crystal mountains, and his face grew worried.

Without warning, he waddled away from the group and faced the distant Crystal Falls Mountain. His tiny wings spread wide, and he took a deep breath.

The sneeze that followed was different. This wasn't bubbles or glitter—this was water. A small stream of silvery liquid that sparkled with magic as it flew through the air and splashed onto the grass.

Bluey stared at the puddle he'd made with wide eyes. Then he tried again. This time, the stream was steadier. A third try made an even better jet of water.

"Look at that," Naomi said quietly. "He's practising."

Embera nodded. "He understands what's at stake. That's the mark of a true guardian—wanting to learn and grow stronger to protect others."

Bluey looked up at the great dragon and chirped once—a sound that seemed to say, "I'm ready to try."

Then he turned back towards the Crystal Falls Mountain.

"The Glitterlings found the crystal first," Embera continued, her voice growing darker. "They love anything that sparkles, and they've hidden it somewhere near the Crystal Falls."

At this news, Bluey's scales flashed even brighter. He made a soft growling sound—barely more than a whisper. Whatever these Glitterlings were, they had something that belonged to him!

"Then we'll get it back!" Kellie said firmly.

Naomi nodded. "Bluey needs it. We have to help him."

"It won't be easy," Embera warned. "The Glitterlings are tricky creatures. But..." She smiled, looking down at Bluey, who was still staring at the mountain. "I think I know just the right helpers for this quest."

Bluey chirped his agreement and took one more practise sneeze, creating a perfect ring of water droplets that hung in the air before falling gently to the grass.

Chapter 4

Whispering Woods

Embera pulled out a rolled piece of parchment. When she spread it out, the map glowed with soft blue light. Tiny moving pictures showed floating islands, sparkling waterfalls, and a dark forest that seemed to wiggle on the page.

"The Whispering Woods are first," she said, pointing to the wiggling forest. "The trees there love riddles. Answer correctly, and they'll let you pass."

Bluey waddled over to Naomi and snuggled against her arms. His scales felt warm, like stones that had been sitting in sunshine.

"What if we get the riddle wrong?" Naomi asked carefully.

The Starling ruffled his feathers. "The trees might keep you there until someone else comes along to try. Could be days. Could be weeks."

"We won't get it wrong," Kellie declared, though her stomach felt a little fluttery.

The path to the Whispering Woods was made of smooth stones that hummed under their feet. Bluey kept trying to catch the musical notes that floated up from each step. Every time he snapped at one, he'd sneeze and create a tiny puddle.

Soon the trees rose up around them like green walls. These weren't ordinary trees. Their leaves shimmered silver and gold, and soft giggles drifted down from the branches. A few leaves broke free and danced in circles

around the girls' heads.

"Visitors!" whispered one tree.

"With a baby dragon!" giggled another.

"How delightful!" laughed a third.

The path ahead was blocked by a bridge made of twisted vines. On the other side, Naomi could see the forest opening up again. But the bridge wouldn't let them cross.

A large oak tree with a face in its bark leaned down towards them. "Answer our riddle, little travellers, and the bridge will hold you up. Get it wrong, and…" The tree's branches rustled with laughter.

"We're ready!" Kellie announced boldly.

The oak's eyes twinkled like stars. "I flow without

moving. I sing without voice. I'm born from the sky but

live in the earth. What am I?"

Naomi's mind raced,

working   through

each   clue

carefully. Flow   without

moving... sing without voice...

born from the sky but live

in the earth.

"Born from the sky." Kellie said, squinting up at the

canopy. "What's born up there?"

"Birds fly there, but they're not born there," Naomi thought aloud.

"Clouds!" Kellie pointed excitedly at a puffy white cloud drifting between the branches. "Clouds are born in the sky!"

"That's it," Naomi said slowly, fitting the pieces together. "And clouds make rain. Rain comes down to earth and..."

While the girls worked on the riddle, Bluey grew restless in Naomi's arms. He wriggled until she set him down, where he began exploring the tree and vines.

When Bluey looked at the path, he saw something that made his scales brighten: a small puddle left by recent rain, sitting in a hollow between the path stones.

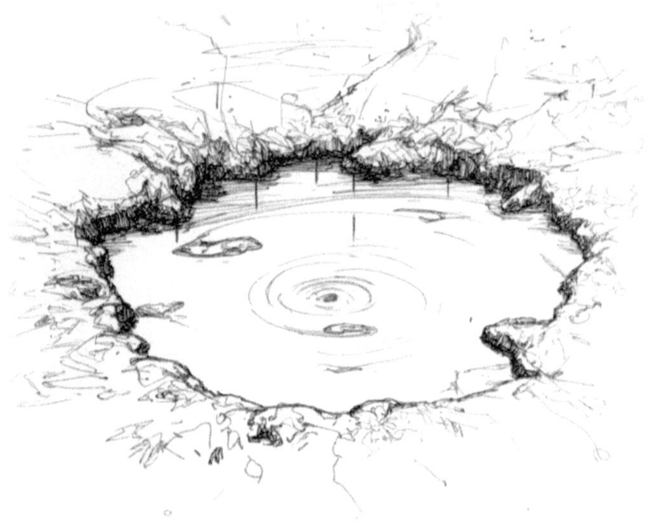

Bluey waddled over to the puddle. He touched its surface gently with one claw, sending ripples spreading outward in perfect circles. The water caught the forest light and threw it back as dancing patterns.

He chirped softly to get the girls' attention, then touched the water again, making more ripples.

"Look at that," Naomi said quietly. "He's trying to help us."

"Flows!" Kellie bounced on her toes. "Water flows!"

Bluey chirped encouragingly and made the water ripple again, more deliberately this time. The motion created tiny waves that lapped at the edges of the puddle.

"But how does it sing without a voice?" Naomi wondered, still working through the riddle.

She thought about the little creek behind her house. "Water babbles over rocks. It makes music, but it doesn't have a mouth to sing with."

Bluey nodded quickly and created another set of ripples.

"And it flows but doesn't really move by itself," Kellie added quickly. "Gravity pulls it!"

"A river!" both girls called out together.

Bluey chirped triumphantly and gave the puddle one last gentle touch, as if to say, "exactly right."

The oak tree's branches swayed like arms clapping. "Correct! The bridge will hold you safe, young riddle-solvers."

The vine bridge straightened and thickened until it looked sturdy enough to hold a full-grown dragon.

Chapter 5

Through the Whispering Woods

Kellie stepped on the bridge first, testing it with one foot. The vines felt as solid as the wooden bridge over Mill Creek back home.

"Come on, slowpoke!" She walked across with her arms stretched out for balance, her red ponytail bouncing with each step.

Naomi followed more carefully, still carrying Bluey.

The little dragon kept trying to lean over the edge to see the glowing flowers far below. Halfway across, he succeeded in wiggling partly free.

"Bluey, no—"

He sneezed. A spray of silvery water droplets scattered everywhere. Where they landed on the bridge, tiny blue flowers bloomed instantly along the vines.

"Oops," both girls said at exactly the same time, then giggled.

"Come on, Bluey." Naomi picked him up again, and they continued walking.

The deeper woods felt like stepping into a tunnel made of trees. Ancient trunks stretched so high their tops disappeared into misty clouds. Glowing mushrooms the size of dinner plates dotted the forest floor like fallen stars. Some pulsed slowly, as if the forest itself was breathing.

A path of smooth river stones wound between twisted roots that had grown into natural archways. Strange bird calls echoed from above, musical and haunting.

Something rustled in a group of ferns ahead. Both girls stopped walking. A creature about the size of a house cat was moving around in there, but they couldn't see what it was.

"What do you think it is?" Naomi whispered.

"Let's find out!" Kellie said, ready to investigate.

Before either girl could decide what to do, Bluey wriggled in Naomi's arms until she had to set him down. The moment his feet touched the path, he did something surprising.

Instead of hiding behind the girls or staying close, Bluey walked forward towards the rustling ferns. His tiny wings spread slightly, not in fear but in a gesture that seemed almost... welcoming.

"Bluey, wait—" Naomi started.

But the little dragon continued forward, chirping softly as he went. It wasn't a nervous sound or a warning call. It was the kind of gentle noise someone might make when trying to let a shy creature know they meant no harm.

The rustling stopped. Then, slowly, the most unusual creature either girl had ever seen hopped onto the path.

Purple fur covered its plump body, and it had wings like a butterfly's. Its ears were enormous, and its tail ended in a tiny puff of sparkles that left a faint trail as it moved.

The creature stared at Bluey. Bluey stared back, completely unafraid.

Then the little dragon did something remarkable. He sat down on the path, making himself smaller and less scary, and then chirped again.

"A Flutterfur!" the creature announced proudly. "That's me! Pip the Flutterfur, to be precise."

"Hello, Pip," Naomi said politely, amazed at how Bluey had talked with Pip.

"Where are you going?" Pip asked.

"To the Crystal Falls," the girls said together.

Pip's wings fluttered excitedly.

"You're going the wrong way for sure. Everyone knows the Crystal Falls are behind you, not ahead of you."

Kellie pulled out Embera's glowing map and spread it on a flat stone. The blue light showed their current location as a pulsing golden dot. According to the map, the Crystal Falls were definitely ahead, through the woods and past a meadow of singing grass.

"The map says we're going the right way," Kellie said confidently.

"Bah! Maps!" Pip dismissed this with a wave of one tiny paw. "Maps lie worse than funhouse mirrors. I've lived in these woods for three whole months, which makes me practically ancient. I know every tree, every stone, every dewdrop! Follow me instead!"

The Flutterfur bounded towards a narrow side path that led into much darker woods. Twisted branches formed a tunnel so thick  with shadows that Naomi couldn't see where it ended.

"I don't think that's right," Naomi said carefully, though she tried to sound kind. "The map seems pretty clear."

Pip's enormous ears drooped like wilted lettuce. His sparkling tail-puff dimmed to barely a glimmer. "But I wanted to help somebody for once. Nobody ever lets me help with anything important."

Bluey, who had been watching, made a decision. He waddled over to the sad Flutterfur and sat down right beside him, close enough that their fur and scales were touching. Then he made a soft trilling sound and very gently nuzzled Pip's drooping ear with his snout.

It was clearly a gesture of comfort and friendship, and Pip's eyes brightened.

"You can help us!" Kellie announced, her face

lighting up with an idea. "What do you know about Glitterlings?"

Bluey chirped approvingly and gave Pip an encouraging nudge.

Chapter 6
Pip's Warning

Pip's ears perked up so fast they made tiny whooshing sounds. His tail-puff brightened to a cheerful pink glow.

"Glitterlings! Oh, I know about them, all right." He hopped in a circle, leaving sparkly footprints on the moss. "Terrible little thieves, they are. No bigger than your thumb, but fast as lightning bugs."

"Where do they hide the things they steal?" Kellie asked.

"Behind the Crystal Falls, in the Shimmer Caves."
Pip's backwards wings fluttered. "But you don't want
to go there. They set traps for big folk like you."

Naomi picked up Bluey, who was trying to catch one
of Pip's sparkly footprints. "What kind of traps?"

"Sticky spider webs that aren't made by spiders.
Holes covered with leaves that drop you into mud pits.
And worst of all..." Pip's voice dropped to a whisper.
"They throw glitter bombs."

"Glitter bombs?" both girls asked together.

"Makes you sneeze for hours." Pip demonstrated
with three tiny sneezes that sounded like a mouse with
hiccups. "Can't see, can't think, can't do anything but

achoo-achoo-achoo."

Bluey tilted his head and let out a small sneeze of his own. A few water droplets landed on Pip's fur, making it shimmer even more.

"Your little dragon's got the right idea," Pip said admiringly. "Water washes glitter right off."

The Flutterfur bounded ahead on the stone path, then stopped and looked back. "I could show you

the secret way to the falls. The safe way."

Naomi and Kellie exchanged glances. The map still glowed brightly when pointed towards the main path. But Pip seemed like he only wanted to be helpful.

"What makes your way safer?" Naomi asked.

Pip's chest puffed with pride. "I found a tunnel the Glitterlings don't know about. Goes right under their lookout posts. Comes up behind the falls where they keep their best treasures."

A distant sound drifted through the trees. High-pitched giggling, like wind chimes made of tiny bells. It was coming from the direction of the main path.

The moment the giggling reached their ears, Bluey went completely still in Naomi's arms. His golden eyes grew wide and alert, and his tiny head turned towards the sound with focus.

"That's them," Pip whispered urgently. "They've spotted something shiny on the regular route."

Bluey looked down at himself and seemed to realise the problem. His scales had been glowing brighter throughout their journey, pulsing with warm blue-green light. In the shadows of the forest, he stood out like a living lantern.

The little dragon nodded, knowing he had to do something. He closed his eyes tightly and concentrated with all his might. Slowly, gradually, his glow began to dim. It was clearly hard work—his tiny body shook with the strain, and his breathing was quicker.

"Look at that," Naomi whispered. "He's trying to hide his light."

But it was difficult magic for such a young dragon. The glow would fade for a few seconds, then flicker back to brightness despite his best efforts. Sweat beaded on his tiny forehead as he struggled to control something that seemed as natural to him as breathing.

The giggling grew louder and more excited.

"Shiny! Shiny somewhere close!"

"Find the sparkly thing!"

"Make it ours!"

"It's probably your dragon's scales catching the light," Pip said. Through the trees, tiny flashes of silver could be seen darting between the branches like flying coins.

B l u e y ' s concentration broke as he heard the Glitterlings getting closer. His scales flashed back to full brightness, and he made a frustrated chirping sound. He'd tried his best, but he wasn't strong enough yet to fully control his glow.

"We need to move," Kellie said decisively. "Right now."

"But is the tunnel really safe?" Naomi wondered.

The giggling grew louder, and now they could hear tiny voices getting more excited.

"This way!" Kellie decided, trusting Pip's plan.

"I hope you know what you're doing, Pip," Naomi said, following despite feeling worried.

Chapter 7

The Secret Tunnel

The giggling got closer, echoing through the ancient trees like silver bells in a windstorm. Through gaps in the canopy, tiny flashes of silver and gold darted between the branches.

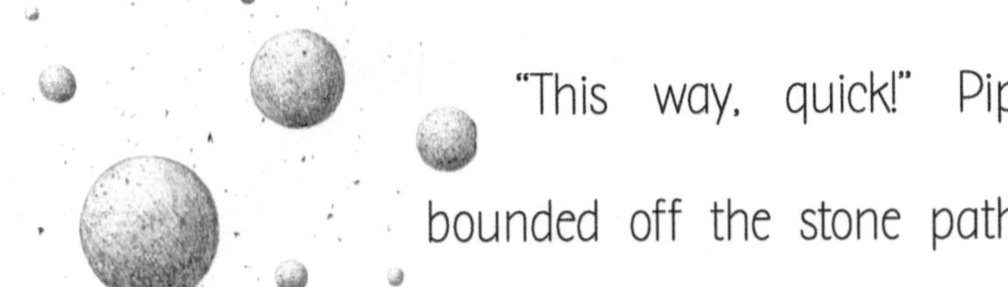

"This way, quick!" Pip bounded off the stone path

towards a cluster of enormous ferns.

Instead of clinging to Naomi, Bluey wriggled out of her arms and dropped to the ground. But he didn't run ahead or lag behind. Instead, he put himself between the girls and the Glitterling sounds, his tiny wings spread out like a shield.

"Bluey, come on!" Kellie called, reaching for him.

The little dragon shook his head firmly. He then c h i r p e d something that sounded like "you first." He pointed with one claw towards the ferns where Pip had gone, then looked towards where the giggling sounds were coming from.

Little glitter bombs zinged above them. Each one exploding against tree trunks in puffs of golden sparkles.

"They found us!" Kellie yelped, ducking.

"Shiny dragon! Pretty scales! Get the shiny!" called tiny voices from the canopy.

Only then did Bluey leave his spot. He scampered after the girls, but kept looking back to make sure the Glitterlings weren't getting too close.

Naomi pushed through the thick ferns and found

the narrow crack in the mossy ground. "Are you sure this is safe?" she called down to Pip's voice below.

A glitter bomb whistled past her ear, answering her question. She dropped through the crack feet-first, with Kellie tumbling down right after her.

"That was close!" Kellie exclaimed as they landed on soft sand.

Bluey landed last in the underground space. He wasn't scared at all and started to look around. His golden eyes swept the tunnel, taking in the glowing moss, the smooth walls, the path ahead.

Above them, the Glitterlings chittering echoed through the crack as the sounds of their tiny wings hummed.

"Where did they go?"

"Sparkly gone."

"Need more glitter. Ooh, look! Another sparkly thing!"

Below in the tunnel, they heard the tiny voices fade

away as the Glitterlings chased after something else.

"That was lucky, Pip," Kellie said.

"Glitterlings get distracted easily," Pip explained,

scampering ahead with his tail-puff bobbing like a

purple lantern. "They likely saw some dewdrops or a

shiny beetle."

The tunnel stretched ahead into darkness, lit only by

patches of glowing moss. The natural light was dim and uneven, leaving pools of shadow that made it hard to see where they were stepping.

Bluey looked around and made a decision. He breathed in and sneezed at the nearest patch of moss. His silvery water splashed against it, and immediately the moss began to glow much brighter, spreading its light in ripples along the tunnel wall.

"Look at that," Naomi said with wonder. "He's lighting the way for us."

"That's brilliant!" Kellie said, clapping her hands.

But Bluey wasn't finished. Every few steps, he would aim another sneeze at a patch of dim moss. He

seemed to know how much water to use to make the light, but not so much that there were puddles of water or make him sleepy.

Pip looked back. "Smart little dragon. That water's got real magic in it, and he knows how to use it."

The tunnel sloped downward, and the air grew cooler and damper. Instead of growing tired from his lighting efforts, Bluey seemed to gain energy as they went deeper. His scales glowed more brightly, and his steps became more confident.

When Naomi's legs started to ache from the walking, Bluey noticed. He waddled over and gently nudged her hand with his snout, then chirped—a sound that seemed to say "we're almost there, keep going."

"Thanks, little guy," Naomi said, feeling better.

"How much farther?" Kellie asked.

Sure enough, just when the tunnel felt endless, a distant roaring sound reached their ears.

"The falls," Naomi whispered.

"We made it!" Kellie said excitedly.

Bluey's scales flashed with excitement, and he gave one final, and very bright sneeze at the moss ahead of them. The path lit up all the way to where the tunnel curved towards its end.

Chapter 8
The Crystal Falls

The tunnel opened onto a ledge of smooth black stone. Water fell from high above and crashed into a pool below. The pool sparkled and made little rainbows in the air.

"Oh my," Naomi breathed.

"This is INCREDIBLE!" Kellie shouted over the loud water.

"The Crystal Falls," Pip said proudly. "The prettiest sight in all of Dreyana. And the loudest too!"

The mist was everywhere. It soaked their clothes and hair right away.

But it wasn't cold like regular water. It felt warm and tingly.

Naomi wiped the water drops from her face and licked her lips. "It tastes sweet! Like honey water."

Behind the rushing water, she could see the dark opening of a cave. Tiny lights flickered inside like fireflies.

"That's where they keep all the stolen things," Pip

explained loudly. "The Shimmer Caves. But getting past the waterfall is hard."

When Bluey stepped onto the dry part of the ledge, something special happened. The little dragon went very still. His golden eyes stared at the cave behind the falls. His scales began to pulse like a heartbeat.

"What is it, Bluey?" Naomi asked.

Bluey didn't answer. Instead, he walked slowly to the edge of the ledge. He spread his tiny wings for balance. He tilted his head like he was listening to something.

"I don't hear anything," Pip whispered. "Do you?"

The girls shook their heads.

When Bluey reached the edge where the spray was thickest, he stopped. He stared at the wall of water. His tail moved once, twice, then stayed still.

"Do you see something in there?" Kellie asked. She crouched down beside him.

Bluey didn't move for a long time. Then he turned to the girls. He looked different now. More serious. Like he understood something important.

The little dragon walked back to Naomi. He tugged at her sleeve with one claw. When she looked down, he

pointed at the waterfall. Then he pointed at himself.
Then at the cave.

"I think he's trying to tell us something," Naomi said.

Bluey nodded. Then he went back to the edge and sneezed. A thin stream of silvery water shot out. It sparkled with magic. Bluey aimed it right at the waterfall.

Where his magic water hit the falls, the water began to wiggle and shimmer.

"Look!" Kellie said. "I think he knows he can move the water!"

"Amazing!" Pip gasped. "I've never seen anything like that!"

Bluey looked back at them and chirped once. It sounded like "yes." Then he turned back to the falls. He planted his feet firmly on the stone. His whole body began to glow brighter.

"But Bluey," Naomi said, kneeling beside him. "That's a very big waterfall. Are you sure you can do it?"

The little dragon looked up at her. He made a soft trilling sound. He spread his tiny wings wide and faced the big waterfall. For a moment, he looked very small next to all that water. Then his scales flashed bright blue-green.

He took a very deep breath. His chest puffed out. His wings shook. Even his tail spread wide. This wasn't just

a sneeze. This was Bluey, using all his magic.

"Here he goes," Pip whispered. His ears stood straight up.

When Bluey let out his power, something beautiful happened. A stream of bright silver water flowed from him. It was steady and controlled. It hit the waterfall exactly where he aimed.

Slowly, the falling water began to m o v e aside. It was like curtains opening. The gap got bigger until it was wide enough for a person to walk through. Bluey held very still. His small body shook with effort, but he didn't stop.

Behind the moved water, the cave opening waited. The dancing lights inside looked brighter now.

"The crystal," Naomi said quietly. "It's calling to him."

Bluey's ears moved when she said 'crystal.' But he didn't break his focus. Sweat appeared on his tiny forehead. But his magic water stream never stopped.

"Now!" Kellie called out. "He's keeping it open for us!"

She ran through the gap. Her feet splashed in warm water. Naomi picked up Bluey gently. He was breathing hard, but his eyes sparkled with pride. Pip squeaked and ran between Naomi's feet as they reached the cave.

As soon as they were inside, Bluey's magic stopped. He slumped in Naomi's arms, very tired but happy. Behind them, the waterfall crashed back together with a loud BOOM.

"You did it," Naomi whispered. She stroked his tiny head. "You got us in here."

"That was the most amazing thing I've ever seen!" Kellie said.

"Better than any magic I know!" Pip added, his tail glowing bright purple with excitement.

Bluey chirped softly. But he was already looking deeper into the cave. Even though he was tired, his scales kept pulsing with that strange beat.

When the mist cleared from their eyes, they could see inside the cave. It looked like the inside of a giant jewellery box. The cave went back very far. Crystals covered every wall and made them sparkle.

But it wasn't just the cave crystals that made Bluey's eyes grow wide. There were piles of stolen things everywhere. Coins, mirrors, marbles, jewellery, and lots of other shiny objects.

And there, right in the middle of the biggest room, sat something special. It was on a stand made of white

crystal. A crystal the size of a ball, glowing with the same blue-green light as Bluey's scales. It pulsed like a heartbeat.

Bluey wiggled in Naomi's arms. He reached toward it. This wasn't just any pretty crystal. This was part of him. The piece that would make him whole.

"The Tide Crystal," Naomi said softly.

"That must be it!" Pip whispered in wonder.

But as Naomi took her first step toward it, a hundred tiny voices began to giggle from the shadows above.

Chapter 9

Dance of Waves

Hundreds of creatures no bigger than Naomi's thumb dropped from the crystal ceiling. They had gossamer wings that caught the cave's rainbow light and grins on their tiny faces. Each Glitterling clutched a handful of glitter like a miniature snowball.

"Intruders!" squeaked one.

"Thieves!" chirped another.

"They want our pretties!" shrieked a third, doing a loop-de-loop in the air.

The Glitterlings began to circle the girls like a glittering tornado. Pip dove behind a pile of golden spoons and covered his big ears.

"We're not thieves!" Kellie said, stepping forward. "That crystal belongs to our friend."

She pointed at Bluey, who had been looking at the Tide Crystal. At her words, he turned to face the swirling Glitterlings.

The leader of the Glitterlings, who wore a tiny crown made of bottle caps, zipped down to hover in front of Kellie's nose. "Everything shiny belongs to us! Pretty shiny, always miney!"

At those words, Bluey stepped forward. He puffed himself up, and the girls thought he looked bigger than when he hatched. With a wiggle, he spread his wings out as far as they could go. He looked right at the crowned Glitterling. His scales flashed brighter than ever.

Then Bluey opened his mouth and let out a roar.

It wasn't the big, earth-shaking roar he would make when grown, but it was the sound of someone claiming what was rightfully theirs.

The sound echoed through the crystal caves, bouncing off the walls. Every Glitterling stopped circling and stared at the tiny dragon in shock.

"But you didn't find it," Naomi said, following Bluey's lead. "It was dropped by accident."

"Yeah, the Starling of Tides didn't mean to drop it. It's still Bluey's," Kellie added.

"Still ours!" the c r o w n e d Glitterling insisted, but her voice sounded less certain now. She threw a glitter bomb at them.

Golden sparkles exploded across Naomi's face. She immediately started sneezing. Achoo! Achoo! Achoo! The other Glitterlings cheered and prepared their own glitter balls.

When Naomi got hit with glitter, Bluey knew he had to help. He waddled quickly over to her. He took a big breath and sneezed.

This sneeze was different. Instead of a big splash, Bluey made a gentle mist. It settled on Naomi's face like soft rain. The water washed all the glitter away without getting in her eyes.

"Thanks, Bluey," Naomi gasped, wiping her eyes with the sleeve of her jacket.

But Bluey wasn't finished. He turned back to the Glitterlings. His scales pulsed with steady light.

"You will not hurt my friends. And that crystal belongs to me!" Bluey said.

The Glitterlings stopped circling. Pip popped up from his hiding place and the girls smiled at each other.

"Water magic," whispered the crowned one. "Real water magic."

"Bluey isn't just any dragon!" Kellie moved her arms like ocean waves. "He's a Tide Dragon, guardian of all the waters in Dreyana!"

The Glitterlings' eyes grew as big as the moon.

"Without his crystal, the oceans will overflow," Kellie

continued, still swaying. "All your beautiful treasures will be washed away!"

Naomi caught on quickly. She began to move her hands like Kellie. "The caves will flood," she added. "Your glitter will turn to mud."

Pip left his hiding spot too. He began to wave his little furry arms just like the girls were.

Bluey watched his friends pretend to be ocean waves. He was still wanting to get his crystal. Then he had an idea.

If they wanted to show the Glitterlings what would happen, he could do more than just roar and try to look big and scary. He could show them real water magic.

Bluey began to move like the ocean, too. But his movements were different. He wasn't pretending - he was making real waves.

As he swayed, tiny water drops appeared in the air around him. They floated and spun in circles. He made a long, musical sound, and the water drops began to dance.

The cave walls got wet and shiny. The air sparkled with real ocean magic.

The Glitterlings looked worried now. This wasn't just pretend. This was real magic.

"The water magic is strong," the leader whispered. "Stronger than our need for pretties."

She looked at her followers and then at Pip, Naomi, and Kellie.

"Hmmm. Bluey, you girls say? A Tide Dragon, you say? Hmmm. Maybe," she said, "we could make a trade."

Chapter 10

A Shiny Deal

The crowned Glitterling flew around the Tide Crystal three times. The other Glitterlings gathered around their piles of shiny things and whispered to each other.

"We need sparkly things," the leader said. "Always need more sparkly things."

"I have something!" Naomi said. She pulled out three chocolate coins from the Easter hunt. They were wrapped in gold foil. The shiny foil made the Glitterlings gasp. "These are special. Magic coins from the human world."

Kellie watched the Glitterlings stare at the shiny foil. Then she had an idea. She reached up and pulled the scrunchie from her ponytail. Her red hair fell loose around her shoulders. The scrunchie was covered in tiny sequins that sparkled in the crystal light.

"And this has lots of little sparkly bits," she added.

Pip bounced excitedly, his tail glowing bright purple.

"I know where there's a whole field of dewdrops that sparkle like diamonds every morning!"

The crowned Glitterling flew between all the offerings. Her wings beat so fast they hummed. She looked at each thing carefully. The chocolate coins clinked together. The scrunchie caught the light and threw sparkles on the cave walls. Pip's dewdrop idea made the other Glitterlings squeal with joy.

While they talked, Bluey had moved closer to his crystal. He wasn't just standing there. He was looking at it very carefully. His golden eyes reflected its blue-green light. As he got closer, the crystal pulsed stronger.

Suddenly, Bluey looked right at the crowned Glitterling. "That's my crystal. I need to take it home."

"These are special things you've never seen before," Naomi said.

Kellie nodded and stepped towards the leader. "Can't you hear it? The ocean is calling to him. He needs the crystal."

Everyone in the cave went quiet. Through the loud waterfall, they could hear a distant sound. It was like whale songs mixed with wind chimes. Beautiful and sad.

The crowned Glitterling's face changed. Her grin went away. She flew to the Tide Crystal and put both tiny hands on it. Then she looked back at Bluey.

"The water magic is strong," she whispered. "Stronger than our need for pretty things."

She turned to the other Glitterlings. "What do you think, my sisters? Should we trade the big crystal for many small treasures?"

The Glitterlings started talking excitedly. Some wanted the chocolate coins. Others wanted to know more about the dewdrop field. Several argued over who would get the sparkly scrunchie first.

"They're really thinking about it," Naomi said hopefully.

"Come on," Kellie whispered. "Say yes!"

The leader held up one tiny hand. Everyone got quiet. "We accept your trade. But you must carry the crystal to the shrine yourselves. We are too small for such heavy work."

"Deal!" Kellie said right away.

"That seems fair," Naomi agreed.

"Perfect!" Pip added, his wings flapping with joy. "I can guide you there!"

"Thank you," Bluey said. He followed it with a few chirps. "Come on, friends. Let's go home."

Chapter 11

A Path in the Sky

The Tide Crystal was heavier than it looked. Naomi and Kellie took turns carrying it as they climbed out of the cave. Bluey walked with them, leading the way.

Every few steps, Bluey would stop and tilt his head. He listened to something only he could hear. Then he would point with one claw to let them know where they should go.

"This way," Bluey said. "The path is safer here."

"I don't know how he does it," Pip said, bouncing

along behind them. "But he's better than any map!"

When they reached a fork in the rocky trail, Bluey

didn't wait. He walked to the right path and looked

back at them. "This way! Come on."

The girls followed. "Good thing he didn't pick the left

path," Pip said as he flew just above the girls' heads.

"Look - it ends at a cliff!"

"Look at that." Naomi pointed as Bluey went around

another rock with sharp edges. "He knows the way to

keep us safe. I think he can feel where the shrine is."

"That's so cool!" Kellie said. "He's like a compass!"

"A very smart compass," Pip added.

"Come on!" Bluey said and kept walking. His scales glowed brighter with each step toward home.

Outside the falls, the mist had cleared. Above them was something amazing: a path made of golden steps and way up a high they changed to clouds.

"The Sky Path," Pip said, standing up tall. "It goes straight to the Tide Shrine."

The cloud path started at

a rocky ledge high above their heads. Golden steps,

shiny like sunlight, curved up the cliff.

"Wow, let's go," Kellie said. She handed the crystal to

Naomi and grabbed the first step. It held her weight.

"This is the best part yet!"

Naomi held the crystal with both hands. Bluey

spread his wings and

began   to   fly

alongside   them

as they climbed.

The little dragon

got very excited.

His   wings

fluttered happily as he flew through the sky for the first time.

"I hope these steps hold me," Pip worried, testing the first one with his paw.

Step by step, they climbed toward the clouds. The golden stairs made music under their feet. Each step made a different note. Bluey began to hum along with the pretty sounds.

Pip climbed behind them. "These steps are slippery!" he called. "But they're holding!"

After climbing all the golden steps, they reached the cloud path. The clouds felt like walking on thick cotton. They bounced a little with each step. To their left, other floating islands drifted by. Dragons of every size and colour flew between them.

"Look at all those dragons!" Pip didn't know where to point first.

The first dragon to notice them was a big silver dragon with shiny wings. She flew close. "Welcome, little Tide Dragon! The oceans have been waiting for you!"

Before, Bluey might have hidden away. Instead, he lifted his head up high and answered back. "Thank you! I'm ready to help." His voice sounded small in the vast area. The silver dragon made a happy trill sound.

More dragons began to fly alongside them. A green dragon called out, "Well done finding your crystal!" A blue dragon with fins like Bluey's said, "We're excited to meet you!" Each time, Bluey answered back. He wasn't shy anymore.

"He's really talking with them," Naomi said.

"Like he belongs here," Kellie said.

"He does belong here," Pip said. "This is his home."

Ahead, the cloud path curved toward the biggest floating island yet. At the top was a building that looked like it was made from one giant pearl. Water flowed from it in gentle streams that fell into the sky.

"The Tide Shrine," Naomi said softly.

"We made it!" Kellie said.

"Finally!" Pip cheered, doing a little flip.

The shrine's pearl walls showed every colour of the rainbow. As they got closer, Bluey began to glow so brightly that Naomi had to squint.

When a group of young dragons about Bluey's size flew down to welcome them, Bluey spoke clearly to them. "Hello! I'm Bluey."

At the shrine's entrance, was a stand with a hollow in the same shape as the Tide Crystal.

"This is it," Naomi said quietly.

"We're so happy for you, Bluey," Pip said. "And for all of Dreyana, too."

"I'm ready," Bluey said. "Thank you for helping me get here."

Chapter 12
The Tide Dragon

At the shrine's entrance was a stand made of white pearl. Its surface was smooth except for one hollow that matched the Tide Crystal perfectly.

Naomi walked carefully toward it, holding the heavy crystal. But as she lifted it toward the hollow, Bluey spoke softly.

"Wait," he said gently.

The little dragon had stepped onto the pearl floor of the shrine. For a long moment, he just looked at the stand.

"This is really it, isn't it?" Pip whispered.

Slowly, Bluey walked to the stand. He put one tiny claw on its smooth surface. Right away, the whole shrine started to change. The pearl walls began to hum softly. The water flowing from the shrine started moving faster.

"Whoa!" Pip gasped. "It's responding to him!"

Then Bluey turned around to face his friends. In that moment, he looked less like the tiny baby dragon they had found and more like the grown-up guardian he was meant to be.

"Bluey?" Naomi whispered.

The little dragon looked at each of them. First Naomi, who had been kind. Then Kellie, who had been brave. And finally, Pip, who had been helpful.

"I understand what this means," Bluey said. "I choose this. I'm ready."

He looked at Naomi. "Please put the crystal in. It's time."

"Oh my," Pip breathed, his tail glowing softly. "He really is ready."

Naomi's hands shook a little as she lifted the Tide Crystal over the hollow. The crystal seemed to jump from her fingers into the hole. It settled in place with a soft ring that echoed through the shrine.

The shrine began to sing.

It started as a low hum in the pearl walls. Then other sounds joined in. It built into music that sounded like waves on the beach, like rain on water, like whale songs in the deep ocean.

"Listen to that!" Pip whispered in amazement. "It's the

most beautiful music I've ever heard!"

Bluey walked to the centre of the shrine and sat down. The magical music swirled around him. He closed his eyes and spread his tiny wings wide. He wasn't scared or excited. He was peaceful, like someone coming home.

"I'm ready to become who I'm meant to be," Bluey said softly.

The change started gently. His scales shifted from blue-green to deep ocean blue to silvery white like sea foam. Each colour flowed like water across his body. His wings got bigger with each breath, becoming strong and beautiful.

"Look at his wings," Kellie whispered.

"They're growing!" Pip said excitedly. "He's becoming magnificent!"

As his wings grew, his tail got longer too. It developed pretty patterns that looked like flowing water.

Light began to shine from the crystal, shooting up into the sky in a bright blue-green beam that could be seen all across Dreyana.

The biggest change was in Bluey's eyes. When he opened them, they were a deep blue.

"Your eyes," Naomi gasped. "They're so beautiful."

"I can feel everything," Bluey said in wonder. "All the oceans, all the tides, all the islands. I can feel it all."

Bluey lifted his head and made a sound unlike anything he had made before.

It started as a roar, but became a song. It rolled across the sky like musical thunder.

"I will protect these waters," Bluey sang out clearly. "I will keep the tides flowing and the islands safe. This is my choice."

"Look!" Pip pointed toward the horizon. "The seas are calming down! The islands are moving back to where they should be! He's really doing it! He's becoming the guardian Dreyana needs!"

Every dragon in Dreyana answered back. Their voices joined his in a huge chorus. "Welcome, Tide Dragon!" the voices called across the sky.

When the music stopped, Bluey looked at his friends. He moved like flowing water now. When he breathed, tiny waves moved through the air around him.

"You did it," Naomi said. "You chose to become who you were meant to be."

"I did," Bluey said with a warm smile. "And I couldn't have done it without you."

Bluey came over and gave them each a hug.

"And I'll remember you too, Pip," Bluey said. "You

helped me find my way."

"You're not just a dragon anymore, Bluey," Pip said. "You're the guardian of all the waters of Dreyana."

"I'll always be your friend," Bluey promised. "No matter how big my job gets."

Embera's wings announced her arrival. The golden dragon landed beside the shrine, her eyes shining with happy tears.

"Well done, young guardian," she said. "The tides of Dreyana flow right once more."

Chapter 13

Home Again

Bluey looked at his friends with his deep blue eyes. He reached up and gently pulled two small scales from his chest. They glowed like tiny moons.

"For you to remember me," he said, placing one in each girl's palm.

When Naomi held hers up to the light, it sparkled with all the colours of the ocean.

"Oh, Bluey," Naomi said. "You're really staying here, aren't you?"

"Yes," Bluey replied. "This is my home now. But I'll never forget you."

His scales felt smooth and magical as Naomi and Kellie held them tightly in their hands.

"I knew we'd have to say goodbye," Kellie said. "But it's still hard."

"It's hard for me too," Bluey admitted. "You helped

me become who I'm meant to be."

"Will you be happy here?" Naomi asked.

Bluey looked at the beautiful shrine and floating islands, then back at her. "I will be. This is where I belong." He pressed his nose against Naomi's hand and let out the tiniest sneeze. Not water this time, but something that felt like ocean mist mixed with starlight.

Where the mist touched her skin, Naomi felt warm and happy. Like floating in calm water on a perfect day.

"But I'll miss you too," Bluey said gently.

Kellie held out her hand, and Bluey gave her the same gentle sneeze. The happy-sad feeling filled her chest.

"We'll miss you too," Kellie said. "But you're going to take care of all the oceans, right?"

Bluey sat up straight and puffed out his chest. "I will protect the waters of Dreyana," he said proudly. "That's my promise."

"Goodbye, Pip," the girls said. "Thank you for helping us."

"Take care of Bluey for us," Kellie added.

Pip ran over and gave each girl a hug. "I'll look after him for you. Make sure he doesn't get into trouble with those big wings."

"Hey!" Bluey protested, batting at Pip with one claw. Everyone laughed.

The Starling of Tides landed beside them. His feathers were neat and tidy now. "Ready to go home?" he asked. "I promise not to get distracted this time."

Embera wrapped her tail around them all.

"Friendship like yours doesn't end," she said. "Every time the tides turn, Bluey will feel your love. And you'll feel his."

Naomi looked at the scale in her hand. "When you hold that near water and think of him," Embera explained, "Bluey will know. And maybe you'll hear him thinking of you too."

Bluey walked to where water flowed from the shrine. He touched it with one claw, and it began to glow. Then he looked back at his friends.

"I'm practising," he said with a small smile. "I've got much to learn about magic and water."

The girls stood up. They each gave Bluey one last hug.

"Goodbye, Bluey," Naomi said.

"Take care of the tides for us," Kellie added.

"I will," Bluey promised. "And thank you. For everything."

Bluey spread his wings wide, catching the light like water. He took flight and did a perfect loop in the air before landing beside them.

"I'm getting better at flying," Bluey said with a grin.

The Starling spread his wings, and the wind began to swirl. The girls held tight to their scales as water drops danced in the air.

"Hold tight to your memories too," Embera called. "They're just as special as those scales."

As the wind grew stronger, Naomi and Kellie kept their eyes on Bluey. The dragon sat at the edge of the shrine, watching them.

"Goodbye, my friends!" he called out. "Thank you for helping me find my way home!"

When the spinning stopped, they were back in Burton Park. Mrs Carson was still reading her newspaper. The fountain bubbled peacefully in the morning sun.

Their Easter basket sat beside them, full of chocolate eggs. The scales in their hands continued to glow.

"Best Easter egg hunt ever," Kellie said with a smile.

Naomi nodded and squeezed her scale gently. From the fountain nearby, she heard the faintest sound of music.

Somewhere far away, a young Tide Dragon was learning to fly. And every time water moved anywhere, two friends would remember.

www.ingramcontent.com/pod-product-compliance
Lightning Source LLC
Chambersburg PA
CBHW020528120726
47904CB00003B/1007